Where We've Been

Editors

Lois Rosen

Jean Rover

Where We've Been

Copyright © 2019
Blue Agate Press
Salem, Oregon

ISBN: 13: 978-0996713016 (Blue Agate Press)

ISBN: 10:0996713018

Cover art: Cynthia Herron, *Lake and Small Boat*, 16" x 16" oil and cold wax on wood with wood carving. To learn more about Cynthia's work, visit: www.cynthiaherron.com

Manufactured in the United States of America

"Writing as an art form belongs to all people, regardless of economic class or educational level ... A writer is someone who writes."

—Pat Schneider, *Writing Alone and with Others*

CONTENTS

POETRY

FICTION

NONFICTION

Trillium Writers

Under the leadership of Lois Rosen, Trillium Writers generate new writing in an encouraging environment using the Amherst Writers and Artists Method, pioneered by Pat Schneider (*Writing Alone and with Others*, Oxford University Press, 2003).

We are a community that supports and encourages our desire to create fiction, nonfiction, prose, or poetry. Our group includes both experienced and beginning writers.

Prompts are offered and participants are free to use them or not. We read our writing aloud if we choose and respond as listeners to point out what we find is strong and memorable in each other's work. Together we provide a fun, safe, confidential space in which everyone is free to write and grow their unique voices.

Country Peace and Quiet
by Sara Dinsdale

Ordinary joys of Oregon country life are many, especially peace and quiet. Heather felt certain she would find that here. During the years of hope and disappointment while she worked long and hard to get her own little piece of heaven, she sustained herself with a vision of relaxing on a weathered front porch, just like in the photo of her favorite bluegrass band.

This was her moment. She cradled her canning jar glass of water, settled into a creaky rocker that came with the house and looked around. In front of her, a packed dirt path met the edge of the porch and climbed over two riverstone steps. She loved their rustic feel, though they rocked as she stepped up or down. Yellow-jackets hung around a gap between the stones. On this late August afternoon, the air shimmered above the fields beyond her yard.

Earlier in the day, she signed bank papers for this place that was now hers. Chests and trunks, baskets, boxes and suitcases were unloaded onto the covered back porch. For the first time since childhood, she and her things were all together in the same place. Slowly rocking, Heather leaned back, picturing linen curtains already laundered, starched, and ironed. They'd move in the sweet breeze that she'd felt on her first visit when she was walking around the neglected house, sheds, and barn. That gentle breeze sold her on the place as it broke up late-summer Oregon heat with a caress, not a blast.

Fields completely surrounded her except for the dirt lane that came off the highway into her dried-up yard of shrubs crisped brown. It curved around the porch, ending by an apple tree with curled leaves. There were no other trees in sight and the hot fields pulsed golden with short stubble like her dad's army haircut, stiff and prickly to touch. She liked the glow they cast, saw her place as a jewel surrounded by this color that made everything look hopeful and painted more shade trees into her vision of the future.

The joys of quiet country life are matched by pitfalls, perils and endless demands, which Heather was about to learn. She ignored the hole in the porch floor just below the picture window (all things in good time) and imagined the beautiful white curtains that would soon flutter there in the breeze. She'd finally use her bounty of linen curtains and tablecloths collected from rummage sales and thrift stores for over twenty years. She'd made it through many a bleak spell by collecting embroidered, tatted, lace-edged, openwork, sheer and heavy linen treasures and imagining the women who'd made them. Through the years they were stored in boxes that had been hoisted into truck beds, one move after another without ever being taken out. Heather never wanted to risk losing them in sudden flight nor get her hopes up that any given move would last long enough for her to hang them. She waited for a permanent place to pull them forth into the light. They could be stained, yellowed, or mouse-chewed in all this time, but she remained optimistic. They were her continuity with the past and hope of a fresh start.

A curious neighbor came by earlier, introduced himself as Fred Smiley and yelled out his truck window. He pointed out that the large window frames were falling apart and should be fixed before winter winds and rain. They wouldn't hold a curtain rod in their current disintegration and soon might not support the glass. Oh, and the front porch had other boards about to give way, and the barn would need to be shored up soon if she was going to save it. Then, he drove on down the road with a little wave. Not exactly the friendly country welcome that she'd imagined, but she wouldn't let it shake her triumphant mood.

Heather wasn't discouraged for she had quiet at this moment and peace would follow. There was no city noise to interrupt and wear her down, no one to take her time and energy. She'd be able to read and write far into the night or whenever she wanted. She would find ways to banish mosquitoes, coax spiders outside, and stop the bedroom light from going off and on by itself. She leaned into the rocker, picked up her water glass, and resumed her dream. By this time next year, she'd cook suppers of vegetables grown in the old garden plot, despite what the agent said about needing fences for raccoons and deer. She loved thinking of her very own wildlife right here and would plant enough for them all to share.

Into her reverie came a horrible roar. She looked up to see an apocalyptic vision, an enormous cloud of dust enclosing a green machine roaring toward her from the side yard. As tall as her house, with tires as wide as her car, it hurtled toward her. She gave a little scream and jumped up from the rocker, not knowing which way to run. Then the massive wheels pivoted into a tight right turn and the beast roared away, pulling a churning, thundering implement past her barn and on out into the endless fields. The dust cloud had its own momentum and didn't swerve. It enveloped her and everything around her in a manmade wind. She coughed several times, cleared her throat, and walked over to the side yard. Fifteen feet from the porch, deep tire prints marked the edge of her property.

Heather stood shaken and dusty. For several minutes more she stared out at the pillar of dust moving out of sight down the enormous field, a jagged brown stripe of turned-up earth following the green monster. She returned to the rocker, picked up her water glass, and adjusted her fantasy, lining the yard with tall poplars and dense hedges of laurel, holly, honeysuckle, wild rose. She'd worked too hard and waited too long to be stopped by a little dust.

The Wait

by Lois Rosen

Excerpt from novel-in-progress, *Dog Killer's Daughter*

1961 Portland, Oregon

"Your hens are lucky," Cora said. "They don't know that getting to visit the kitchen isn't going to happen much longer. It's a good thing they can't read the newspapers." Oops. Did Cora need to rub it in and upset her Italian grandmother, Nonna Silvia? *Urban renewal. Urban renewal.* The words were a curse. Urban renewal meant Jewish-Italian-Russian-Negro-Gypsy removal.

That warm June afternoon, Nonna's white kitchen curtains fluttered, showing off their hems, decorated with embroidered chickens. The design perfectly mimicked Aida's multi-layered plumage. Cora gazed at the alluring Aida, who strutted across the red and black-checked linoleum between the gas stove and the kitchen table's chrome legs. The tips of her feathers resembled ink-dipped quills. Cora imagined the dignified hen as a diva, emerging from a theater after an opera performance, dazzling her fans with her ermine-white stole, trimmed midnight black, and glimmering in spotlights, photographers' cameras flashing like sparklers.

Aida and her feathery followers, Musetta and Lola, liked to come calling at Nonna's kitchen for after-school snack-time. Cora wondered if the hens were also Jewish Italians. Besides eating leftover vegetables, they cheerfully chewed their afternoon treat mixed with Italian bread crumbs and kosher matzo meal.

While Nonna sat gripping an embroidery hoop in one hand and a needle guiding black thread in the other, Cora lifted fresh eggs one by one from a basket. She washed the shells with a rag soaked with warm vinegar-water. The smell made her want to hold her nose, but the shells needed to be germfree. She dried each one with a cloth towel, then put it in a cardboard carton on the table. She looked up from her chore to watch Aida's queenly march through the legs of the table, followed by her retinue.

The hens, lucky to be undisturbed by rumors and muttering about forced relocation, waited for the attention each deserved. They didn't have to listen to the complaints Cora heard on the sidewalks, at school, in her kitchen at home, in her building, and at businesses where owners grumbled that the reimbursement money offered was *highway robbery, peanuts, a goddamn insult*. Every time her dad said rich developers were getting away with murder, her body tensed. She wanted to karate chop and kick Syd Feller's desk and the desks of every other Portland Planning Commission mucky muck to smithereens, which was exactly what her home and Nonna's were soon to become: shards, rubble, and ash.

Tears formed in her eyes. The egg in her hand shattered. The yoke and its white splatted on the cleaned eggs, the carton, her hands, the washrag, and on her precious poodle skirt. "Oh crap!"

Aida, Musetta, and Lola squawked their disapproval.

"My skirt's ruined."

"Run to my bedroom. Put on my housecoat. Stains you don't want to leave for long. Hurry," Nonna said.

With the survival of her skirt at stake, Cora rushed to Nonna's bedroom. When Cora and her mom had shopped for the stylish skirt at Meier and Frank, her mom used her own savings from her part-time job, so she wouldn't have to always ask her husband for money. The gray swirl they found, embellished with an appliqued pink poodle sporting curly wool hair, was even cuter than what Cora had dreamed of. Except for shoes, it was her most expensive piece of clothing.

In Nonna's bathroom, she rinsed goo and shell pieces off her hand. The broken fragments made her think of the rubble left on Front Street after bulldozers demolished community buildings. She didn't intend to destroy the egg, not like those bulldozers she kept hearing. The daytime noises echoed in her mind and kept her awake with the terrible banging, clanging, and groaning. The moonscape of destruction was getting closer.

The mirror showed the damage. The poodle's tail and the gray felt background looked like a painting of eggy icicles. She pulled on the waistband. The button ripped off—there was no time to look for it. She yanked the skirt down with one hand, held the other palm under the front fabric to keep it flat, spread the skirt on the bed, grabbed the robe, tied it on. Run. Swathed in aqua terrycloth, she raced to Nonna in the kitchen, the skirt held out on her forearms like a sacrificial offering. It was only a skirt, but it meant a lot more. Money for moving was scarce. How could they afford deposits for new homes with the pittance the city was offering them? The property grabbers called the destruction of a fifty-four block community "eminent domain." The community development people were taking over, buying up homes for way less than they were worth, saying, "Sorry, but this is our best offer."

"I wiped the floor and each egg again," Nonna said. "Many times I took the stains from Nonno's felt hats. We fix this. You don't worry." She had Cora put the skirt down by the long lasagna pan filled with lukewarm water and a container of dish soap. She handed her a clean rag. "Listen, I tell you something about milk, a phrase I learned in English class. After this accident, I say now—'Do not to cry over spilled egg.'" Nonna giggled. "So the skirt front, just the egg part you soak. We must work fast so the stain, it will not stay. We leave it soak long enough. But we cannot rub much or soak the whole skirt. Felt shrinks."

Just the word *shrinks* gave Cora a shrinking feeling in her chest. The skirt might be trashed. And her life.

"You do it now. Softly dip the stained part, dab it with a little drop of dish soap."

Cora did as Nonna said. It seemed too simple, but Nonna knew many simple ways to garden, to cook, and they worked.

"Dab and dab for five minutes. You check your watch. Then you leave the stains in the water. We wait about a half an hour. Later rinse and pat dry. I give you a towel. If you need to do all again, you repeat."

"How many times?"

"Until no more stain. The slow way, the true way."

Cora followed Nonna's advice. She followed the easy directions, dried her hands, and waited. That was the hard part—the waiting. All of her family kept waiting, waiting. It was a waiting game cheaters fixed. Players like herself, Nonna, her parents, the chickens, all of them, held losing cards

She hoped Nonna's advice would work. "Mom will have a fit if the stains are permanent. She hates my spilling, dripping, bumping into things, and now I've ruined her gift to me. I swear she'll holler her head off if she hears I was watching a chicken and forgot what I was doing. She'll be furious if she finds out Aida, Musetta, and Lola were in here. She doesn't believe me when I tell her how tame and well-behaved the ladies are. All she notices is their poop and the odor. She refuses to acknowledge that we always use bleach water after their visits to sanitize the floor."

"For your mother, my hens, they are difficult after the many things she had to do on the farms way up in the Italian hills and in the convent where we hid also during the war. She needed to butcher chickens, though she hated to. It made her feel sick and guilty. Born in Pitigliano, I grow up with farm animals. To me as a little girl, they are friends. I never like to kill them for food, but I accept it. But your mother had not lived that life in Rome."

So when they absolutely had to move from South Portland, there was no point in begging her mom to keep the chickens with them.

Nonna jabbed and pulled her needle through her embroidery.

Cora, done with the five minutes of dabbing, let the stains soak. She poured glasses of water for her and Nonna, and sat across from her at the table.

Meanwhile, Aida stood unmoving, waiting for her chance to be treated with respect. After all, who did that commoner, the girl sitting in the fake leather kitchen chair, think she was? Cora understood the imperious clucking, which in everyday English meant, "Lift me onto your lap. Stroke my downy coat. Do it now."

"Here we go, your Royal Highness," Cora said, as she settled her onto the padded throne Cora's thighs provided. Aida sat upright, dignified, as ever, and alert, surveying the kitchen, her *demesne*—her domain. Cora loved it when a word she'd seen somewhere in British literature popped into her mind. Aida deigned to allow Cora to pet her. The girl dipped her fingers deep into dear Aida's luxurious, layered feathers. You're sure looking splendid," she said, not wanting to think about how bedraggled Aida might look, separated from Nonna and stuck in some crowded metal cage or worse.

She gazed across at her dear Nonna Silvia, again holding an embroidery hoop. "What are you making?"

"Well," Nonna said. "Aida shouldn't get all the notice. Everyone who visits asks me about the curtains. So now I'm making a tablecloth with designs of Musetta and Lola around the edges. You know so well why I need to get it done now while my models I can watch and not hurt their feelings. So soon it is going to be very hard." Nonna lowered her head.

Tears, Cora didn't want to show, were welling in her eyes, too.

Cora told Aida, "Sorry, Your Highness. I gotta get up and give the others a chance." She gently lifted and placed Aida on the floor. Musetta and Lola hovered around Cora's feet waiting for their turn to rule the roost. Aida turned her back on Cora and pecked at Nonna's shoe. The signal understood, Nonna put down her embroidery, stepped to the cutting board, and slipped Aida bits of apple, Aida's fruit treat of the day. For Musetta, melon after her turn on Cora's lap, and for Lola, last but not least, little cubes of red Italian tomato, her signature color, after all.

Nonna sat down again. Cora, coming back to the table from checking on the stain, fading, but not enough, dabbed and left the skirt to soak. Then she peered over Nonna's shoulder and ran a finger along the stitches. "Your black satin threads with their bluish sheen are perfect for Musetta."

Nonna looked up. "The blue-black color makes me think of the clarinet of Benny Goodman, how his instrument sobs and laughs in 'Rhapsody in Blue.'"

"I could listen to that opening a zillion times." Cora said.

"Go ahead, put the portable player on the table here in the middle and play the record."

Cora, of course, didn't need to be told where the portable was nor where to find their favorite 78 of the rhapsody, its album cover with the photos of Toscanini as conductor, Benny Goodman with his passionate clarinet performance that Cora adored, and George Gershwin, so thrilling on the piano. The music spread a bittersweet, syncopated background for the hurried perfection of Nonna's stitching. Cora had learned that the jazz concerto was the first written for and performed by a jazz orchestra. George Gershwin came from a Jewish refugee family, so did Benny Goodman, and look how successful they became. That was something to remember, something about not giving up. They had musical gifts, tremendous talent. She had a mastery of words for someone her age, a talent for debate and speech making. But no matter how many letters she wrote to the city council or signs she made, that hadn't been enough. They'd lost.

Musetta was on the floor right by her feet. The satin-black beauty, as if entranced by the music, accepted her turn on Cora's lap. During one of the times when the crescendo rose to another boisterous da…da da…daaaa, she gently set Musetta onto the floor and picked up Lola. Her ruddy red feathers' iridescent gleam complemented the flashy piano parts played by Gershwin.

"Sad, he died at thirty-eight. Such a talented man. A big loss." Nonna shook her head.

"Yeah, sad." Just the right artist for her and Nonna to listen to.

The music ended. While Nonna lifted the needle, Cora set down lovely Lola and shooed the hens back outside. Time to check her skirt. Stains there, but fainter. There was hope. Finished dabbing again, she left the felt to soak and went back to the table.

"And now?" Nonna asked.

"Getting there." She nodded toward the record player. "Again?"

Nonna put down her embroidery hoop and winked.

"Shall we?" Cora winked back and opened the door between the kitchen and the living room, set the needle in the groove to start, and led Nonna in the space between the davenport and the étagère. Just like Martha Graham, they'd loved watching on TV, they let themselves dance in whatever modern ways the music inspired them to, miming sadness, joy, fear, excitement while they whirled, swayed, extended their arms and legs, their bodies echoing the notes. Their troubles remained, but the record, played louder, drowned out worries, swept aside in the music's grand sweep. But the rhapsody came to its end. The needle rasped.

The final eviction notice hadn't come yet, but it would, and then what?

Not a Professional Ballerina

by Lois Rosen
From *VoiceCatcher*

I'm a kindergartener, showing off my sunset-gold, satin-topped
leotard, with the triple-layered, net tutu, sticking way, way out,

wearing black leather ballerina slippers on the day-camp bus,
where Stanley, our driver grins. "You look beautiful,"

and I bow for my fans. I am the dancer who does not change
into shorts or a bathing suit all day.

~

Finally twelve, promoted to dance *en pointe*, I slip my feet
into pink satin toe shoes. Lambswool puffs caress my toes.

Long pink satin ribbons crisscross my ankles. I teeter on
tippy toes, rising *relevé, pas de bourrée*, and, *assemblée*, aloft.

In the mirrored room, at the barre, I *plié, arabesque*, let go,
float above Mrs. Berliner's live piano's Debussy, Tchaikovsky.

~

Now 71, at Jazzercise—no barre, no mirrored walls, not
one tutu, any old sneakers, ceiling fans to cool hot flashes,

I move to "Uptown Funk," "Love Yourself," "Rock
That Body," and the consolation of "One Call Away."

Stiff and creaky, still I grapevine, *plié, chassé*, as iPod
speakers blare, and walk sassy to "Baby, I'm Worth It."

Always Behind
by Marge French

I'm in my mid-forties at the top of my lucrative career. I'm attractive, confident, poised, intelligent, and popular. People seem impressed with me. They say I have a put-together look.

No one sees my private life. I consistently misplace items or most likely the gremlins get in here and hide them! I can be working on a manuscript, leave the room for ten minutes, return, and the papers have disappeared. Or, sitting at my desk, I get out the postage stamps. While I open the drawer for envelopes, the stamps are gone. Maybe I've covered them with other papers.

Yesterday, I needed a tape measure. I looked three times in my sewing basket and three times in a small box I have for my often-used personal tools like bottle opener, small hammer, pliers, screwdriver, and ice pick. It's not there either.

In desperation, I opened my Pandora's Box, my kitchen junk drawer. It is shocking to see such clutter. I am going to organize it sometime. I wonder if that big pink paper clip is in there. I see string, thumb tacks, teabag holders, wine corks, and scissors. I see those two blue round things that help me open jars, like a grabber maybe. No one is ever around to hear me yell, "Help." I even see things there I don't recognize, things I seldom use and should throw away.

Oh, here's that pink paper clip I couldn't find, but no tape measure. At my wit's end, I finally empty the whole drawer onto the kitchen table. Good grief! What a mess! I see glue sticks, a new eraser, a tube of Duco Cement, nutcracker, those birthday candles I couldn't find for Sue's birthday cake, buttons, instructions for the new faucet, and the ruler that Andy desperately needed last night for his homework assignment. Ah, at the bottom of the pile is that elusive tape measure, right where I hurriedly put it, no doubt.

If there's one thing I don't like, it's for people to be late. I'm seldom late or keep people waiting. I make a special effort to be ready when friends pick me up. I plan to have plenty of time, but at the last minute something always happens. The phone rings. I must answer that call from the doctor's office. I can't decide which scarf to wear or if I want to wear one. I'd better put those breakfast dishes in the sink or dishwasher. I forgot to water the plants for a few days. I need to do that. I become frustrated and tense when I have difficulty putting on my left earring. There's that phone again!

As I recall, last-minute planning has always been a problem. Our home was on the block next to the high school. When the five-minute bell rang, I could hear it and was out the door immediately but always at the last minute.

At the airport in Osaka, I was so enthralled looking at the tempting gifts available that I was in shock to learn that my plane was leaving in fifteen minutes. I finally arrived at boarding, but the line had disappeared. Somehow, someone rushed me onto the plane.

The other day, I got up an hour early to make an appointment on time. I read the paper too long, enjoyed relaxing with Mr. Willaby, my cat, and watched breaking news on TV. On my way to get the mail, I chatted with my neighbor. I had to hurry as usual to keep my appointment!

I often think about changing my ways, so I'll be more relaxed when it's time to leave the house.

Oh well, I'll think about that tomorrow.

Miss Dictionary
by Marge French

"Miss Dictionary. That's what we'll call her," said Alex. "It's ridiculous that we have to take a college course on the dictionary! Since I was in the fourth grade, I knew how to look up words, find the definitions, pronunciation, the accents, and abbreviations. That's enough for me. She says, 'This class will be fun. You'll learn so much and enjoy revealing stories.' Surrounded by books crammed in all three bookcases in the room, she hugs Mr. Webster and says, 'I just love dictionaries.' Can you imagine that? She loves dictionaries."

"Yeah, Alex," said Shorty. "And I'm not going to buy a new dictionary or textbook for this stupid class."

Shorty got his nickname because he's short, usually speaks in short phrases, has a short temper, and is always short of cash. Alex, tall and lean, red-haired and freckled, is enthusiastic, quick to form an opinion, and share it.

One evening Alex and Shorty went to the Blue Onion where students and staff hung out. After a couple of drinks and looking at the girls, they started to leave. "Oh look," said Alex. "Isn't that Miss Dictionary sitting in the corner over there? She's sitting with a man!" He was husky with a black beard and huge gray eyebrows that maneuvered half way up his forehead, quite a contrast to Miss Dictionary with her small foxlike face, long nose, and sunken cheeks. "She has on the same black suit she wears to class. Why didn't she at least wear a bright-colored scarf with it?"

As they continued making disparaging remarks, the music changed and the band started pounding out "Thunderstruck," a really hard-rock tune. Miss Dictionary and her partner dashed out of their seats, stomped their feet and let it rip! They twisted their bodies in all directions, knees bent, twirling, arms flying, shimmying to the floor, reaching to the sky, all the time stomping, stomping.

Alex exclaimed, "Get a load of that!" He threw her in the air out of reach, and she landed on her feet on the floor without losing a beat. "Wow, it's hilarious. She's smiling. She's a hottie."

The music changed to a slow tempo. The man slipped his hand gently on her back and led her to their seats. Smiling and sitting cheek-to-cheek, they joined Nat King Cole in singing "When I Fall in Love."

The next day, Miss Dictionary stood beside her desk as usual, holding a beloved dictionary in her hand wearing her blue suit instead of the black one. Her pulled-back hair made her appear quite stern. "Today we are so excited to learn more about etymology. I chose the word *lamp*. Lamps have changed from very early ones millions of years ago to the fabulous lighting of today."

Alex and Shorty were sitting in the back of the room with friends, yawning and fidgeting. After class Alex said, "I was really interested when she talked about kerosene lamps. When my grandmother was a little girl, her mother had only kerosene lamps for lighting. I can picture this old lady going up the stairs at the old farmhouse to her bedroom with that lamp Miss Dictionary called a finger lamp made with a place to put your thumb. A finger kerosene lamp. Can you imagine that?"

Shorty mumbled something while the others dismissed the comment.

Later that day, Alex and Shorty visited the hospital to see Jacob who had a broken leg from a bad fall in football practice. As they were leaving the hospital, Alex said, "Look in that room. Isn't that Miss Dictionary reading to all those children huddled together and climbing all over her?"

"It's her," muttered Shorty.

"The children love Miss Beverly," a nurse informed them. "She's been coming here twice a week for years. She's a priceless help— reading, taking special care of a child who is having problems. I don't know what we would do without Miss Beverly."

"Can you beat that? She does have a life besides the dictionaries," said Alex.

Shorty replied, "She's still nuts. Anyone whose life is the dictionary is nuts."

The students agreed that the idioms class was actually fun. As laughter drifted across the room, that small group of rude freshmen ambled in a little late and settled down in their usual seats in the back of the room. Miss Dictionary was standing by her desk hugging and loving the *World's Largest Idiom Dictionary*. She had just told them the story behind the idiom "upset the apple cart." When a vendor of apples in early English cities struck a rut or cobblestone, he upset the apple cart. Miss Dictionary reminded her students that idioms often come from the language of a particular group of people or area of a country, and the stories behind them are fascinating. "Your assignment next time, as an individual or a participant in a small group, is to create a possible idiom for this particular technological period using its current unique vocabulary."

As they were leaving the room, Shorty grumbled, "Hold your horses! Why the big rush?"

Alex retorted, "I'm at the end of the rope with you. Step on it."

Alex and Shorty had an assignment at the prestigious DeYoung Museum. Not being particularly familiar with that environment, they put their best foot forward and even wore fashionable sport shirts with their best jeans. After finishing their assignment, they discovered a room filled with portraits. Robert Kennedy, Dr. Martin Luther King, Judy Garland, as well as the current mayor and other local residents surrounded them. The likenesses were excellent, even spectacular. The portraits looked alive, revealing their individual, recognizable characteristics.

At the front of the room stood the featured artist, Miss Beverly Hudson, dressed in a smart, fashionable turquoise suit, soft black leather boots, and sporting a classy modern hair-do. Could it be? Yes, it was Miss Dictionary! Standing proudly beside her was her dancing partner, looking very handsome, wearing well-tailored black pants and a black shirt with a bright turquoise scarf and spectacular turquoise jewelry.

As they examined her self-portrait, it seemed to sparkle. A bright intense light shown on the picture as the real Miss Dictionary appeared to Alex. He exclaimed, "Look! Miss Dictionary's nose is not so long, her face is fuller, and her eyes and mouth are quietly smiling. Her long hair is hanging loosely around her face. She's awesome!"

"I guess so," mumbled Shorty.

The next morning Shorty rushed his roommate out the door exclaiming, "Hurry, I don't want to be late. Let's sit close to the front so we won't miss any of Miss Dictionary's lecture. Today, it's about the technical aspects of the dictionary and how they influence the changing world. You know, I'm beginning to love the dictionary and the talented, caring Miss Dictionary."

Alex grinned. "Me too."

Secrets My Sisters Told Me After We Grew Up
by Nancy Fischer

George, our next-door neighbor, had another wife in Bulgaria.
His U.S. daughter sent his ashes back. *We've had him for over
40 years*, she told her Bulgarian half-sister.
It's only right that you have him now.

Almost everyone, one block over, got divorced.
The street was a cul-de-sac.
Do you think that mattered?

Neighbor Betty, runner-up to Mrs. America—
or so we'd been told—died on a bedpan.
Why does this seem ironic?

Always in the latest fashion, Mary was a shopping addict.
Her husband, a Boeing engineer like our dad, bought her
a lake house, a mountain chalet, and a new car every year.
Who got what in the divorce?

Walt, who with his family joined us for Thanksgiving
and Easter dinners, was known to smack his wife.

In my mom's kitchen I heard the women tell her,
Just don't rile him up. His second wife committed suicide.

Vivacious red-headed, Katy, who always said, *Oh no,*
kid, I just ate, died of a heart starved by anorexia.
We found out after her passing.

Small-for-his-size, Georgie, who we all thought odd,
is in prison for killing his girlfriend's toddler.
His mom, Bunny, was a yeller.
Her husband's a saint, my mom said.

The Japanese family down the street, whose mom
taught us kids to sew, had been interred in WWII.
Why did our parents wait five decades to talk about it?

Bridge
by Nancy Fischer

Bridge mix and salted nuts
were our bribes for being invisible,
five sisters in PJs, playing calm
to our Mom's frantic fury.

While out in the living room, big-bosomed women
in form-fitting dresses with names like Chi Chi and Opal
crowded around green card tables, blowing blue smoke
to the ceiling where it formed its own weather.

Forks clinked on glass plates, near tiny napkins
with black diamonds and red hearts, and note pads
with scribbled code, short pencils with no erasers.

What was this game they played so effortlessly, which we,
the uninitiated, knowing only Old Maid and I Doubt It, tried
to decipher through mumbled laughter and shrieks of surprise?

Duty (and awkwardness) denied us firstborn passage to this
foreign land, while younger ones, excused their wandering
espionage, floated back to us with smears of kisses and perfume,
but no hows or whys.

In the morning, picking up the cold trail
of what remained, I sipped the bitter nectar
from their lipsticked glasses.

Mammy (For Frances Landon, my great grandmother)
by Nancy Fischer

I'm sure if she could, Mammy
would tell me the story of the cross burning
(as she'd been told or imagined)
the Irish Catholic family down the lane,
fright-awakened and pressed behind the door,
her Baptist men folk front-lit by flame,
backlit by history, and "first-come-first served."
A string of ancestors stretched to England.
No errant tangles and loops allowed.
She'd tell me how she'd met *their* boy,
young man, her man, her husband
—how we'd love to hear *that* story!—
The tangling of taboos.

My mom told me that once in town with her aunts,
she saw a woman that *–Hey, looks just like Mammy!*
They shushed her, whispered it was Mammy's sister, Laura.
No, Mammy doesn't have a sister!

But it was Mammy's face, mom's face, and my face.
Could Mammy's brothers and uncles (father?)
even have imagined that their dark night's action
would one day scorch them so completely,
that even in death her ashes remain resolutely apart?

In the green genealogy pamphlet Mom gave me,
with rusted hand-stapled binding, less than two silent
inches separate Mammy and Laura, her only sister.
One can make up anything, when truth is left out.

When Devices Delight

by Karen Runkel

In certain areas of my life I believe I'm spontaneous and still a bit wild. But in others a routine rules, bringing not only comfort but daily pleasures. My Starbucks time, when I walk the two miles with unread portions of the *New York Times* folded and tucked into my purse, is more than just a routine.

There's the exercise, of course, but also the avoidance of distractions. I have a perfectly cozy and comfortable sofa by the fireplace, with a tree-filled view to the east which I've cherished for nearly forty years. But, if I read there, it's too easy to interrupt myself with an unfinished task, a new project, or an unexpected nap.

So off I go to drink my grande Misto—their version of a cafe au lait—on a high stool at the long bar facing the corner of Court and Liberty, one of Salem's centerpiece intersections. As I read, it's a treat to look out every now and then to watch the passing parade, realizing that I'm witnessing views of people and situations repeating themselves all across America.

But it's also the little dramas that delight me. Take these two interactions observed during one week from my regular spot, each so private, so unique. First was a nearby middle-aged woman silently moving hands and fingers toward her cellphone in a truly puzzling manner until, with a flash of insight, I decoded this as Skyping with a deaf friend.

She was intensely signing to the small screen with head nodding, face smiling, fingers making words, oblivious to those around her.

A few days later, again watching the world go by with my coffee and newspaper, I heard soft crooning from a man two seats away. Young and handsome, perhaps Indian or Pakistani, he was engaged in quiet and unintelligible conversation until he suddenly crooned again into his cellphone. Though the words were unfamiliar, it was clearly a love song, caressing and gentle in tone.

Trying not to stare, I was transfixed by such unabashed emotion in this common and public setting.

Each experience also reminded me how set my impressions can be. Why had I not gone beyond the obvious and realized that in one case both parties may have been deaf. In the other, both parties may have been the same sex.

We learn in mysterious ways. We find wisdom in the most mundane places!

Later, walking home, these moments with their small and sweet stories remained with me. Two strangers—and their cellphones—had unknowingly opened my mind and given me a chance, so briefly, to imagine lives far beyond the walls and windows of Starbucks. I considered all the negative opinions and rants about our massive overuse of such devices, the supposed waste of time, the jokes deriding conversations full of triviality . . . and yet I knew there could also be love and magic—and I will be watching, listening, for more.

Four Stories High

by Paul Suter

This prose poem is born from every home I've lived in, every home made, every home I've passed on city streets, every home I've discovered and set up in forests, beside streams, on beaches, near mountain peaks.

"Every day is a journey, and the journey itself is home."
Matsuo Basho, 17th C

Home, with a quiet front yard, a creek out back, a porch and a deck, blends with the land I know. This land, the maples and dogwoods, these gardens, this path through needs me to keep it alive, to remember the snap of a twig, the crunch of dry leaves, the random call of jays, the soft brush of cedars with the wind.

Second home of my young life, remembered for tall windows at the front of house, a view of lawn and sidewalk and street; tall windows at the side, facing a patio, an image of green and orange and purple and red and gray; then of white, the cabana roofline and supports, straight lines, straight like the white lines on a highway leading to heaven. A brick fireplace underneath. Ivy up a little slope to the right, and to the left, more ivy over a fence — and beyond, a driveway that climbs to the neighbors. Radiating out from my home, a neighborhood, a community, a community that I loved and friends I remember from age ten to eighteen. Easy to name, easy to see: Steve, Laurie, Dan, Jimmie, Dickie, Paul, Scot, Dave, Christine, Diane.

Like dreams, home is a vessel that reveals where we've been and how we came to be here (a migration story); what the new place is made of (the environment); how we live here now and prepare for tomorrow (spiritual and ethical).

To the first people of Australia, the land is not just space; it is place, it is home. Land itself has levels of consciousness, known in the dreaming night. Awake, the people know their home place better.

When we know a place, we know how to walk about in it; we know the dreamtime stories of the place, how all the earth, and this place in particular, came to be; we know how the place relates to each person individually.

We carry the feel of home wherever we go. At a coffee spot one day, I need a spoon to squeeze my jasmine pearl green tea bag. I look, can't find one, ask the barista. She points to a drawer marked silverware. I open it and there is a tray just like you would find at home. I say to her, "Just like home." She smiles agreement.

The ultimate home is one that welcomes any and all, especially the homeless — those fleeing trauma or violence, war or famine, climate disasters, or shuttered workplaces.

A drunken young man writhes on the sidewalk, groaning, reaching out a hand. He seems to say, "Got a cigarette." A passerby says, "No," after pausing and listening. The passerby goes to his car, and thinks to himself he has to go back to see how this man is doing. He does, taking his worn fleece sweater to give him if he needs something to keep him warm.

For some, home is a car or van. Two young men arrive at a van in a city parking lot. A third young man comes into the scene, now a fourth. They rummage in boxes and a cooler for sandwich fixings. Finally, one more sign of home, a puppy and its mother come out.

For some, a manufactured home, a mobile home, is home. Manufactured says a little more permanence to place, a more inviting place, more like home.

A good home stands up, stands out, stands tall, stands for something, something real and substantial — and lives to see its one moment, its one day, and maybe no other, but at least it has that one day, that one day seen by a walker, a cyclist, a skateboarder. Seen the way artwork is seen on a gallery wall next to many other paintings poised there, positioned there.

Home cradles memory and fear. In the early light the gift of quiet, at night searching moon-whitened clouds for signs and apparitions. Home records laughter and tears. The time the polenta just didn't turn out to be a hit. Or when a young boy ducked his father's playful jab and the cut above his lip became a scar for life. A story all could wrap themselves in whenever the old house (the boy's first home) was mentioned.

Home holds a mirror up to everyone at one time or another. Getting ready for a job interview, for the first-grade photo, for graduations. Looking at the teary face after the lost game, the speech contestant undone, the friend whose small plane went down.

Home is a lace curtain and potted plants in a couple's first home. It is slants of light through slatted blinds late afternoon, casting barred and thin lines on a painting the couple acquires on their first anniversary.

Home returns our gifts a hundredfold. Home lets us practice our entrances into the world. Home gladly holds secrets and tells stories. Home accepts the vagaries of what we like in the home.

Home strengthens us, even if it tortures us, troubles us, upsets us, rejects or dampens our dreams. If home is harmful, there might be a room of one's own made into the home place; or other homes can be found, and there, what a home is meant to do flourishes when the haunted person speaks, "Enough!"

A home destroyed by fire is viewed with grief and doubt. Can these be overcome? Can doubt be replaced with hope and hope's vision of a new place for the next stages of life? A couple looks on with bitterness and doesn't know where strength will come from to rebuild or to move to a new home. There may be revival, from the ashes, from deep sadness and despair, from the nothing home to a phoenix rising. But the old home stays with them the way a sick or dead family member does.

When all you know is war and camps and fleeing and refugee families, and common kitchens, showers, latrines, and lanterns, and mud and rain, and sun and heat, your thoughts of home squeeze your routine with anger and hurt and worry. You long to return home, to your place, to what made you you. You long to be where you can name the rise of the hill behind your home, where you can hear familiar blue jay calls, where children play hide and seek in familiar places.

Home tells us to feel at home when nothing else beyond helps, supports, nourishes. A refuge. Refugees long for that refuge, the refuge of their home, land and country. What courage to enter a new country, a new land, a new home. Will they be able to make more of this place than just four walls? Will they be able to call the new country and land home? Will they take out the one photo they have of the old place, mother sitting with her grandchild?

When someone is gone from a home, never to return, home fills with the sound of footsteps, the clash of dishes, the brush of hot air from fire or furnace. Home feels strange. Speech is drained. Laughter is singular. Pleasure is pain. Reasoning is told to remain, but refuses the invitation.

We take vacations away from home. Then we return home — and that satisfies, comforts, feels right. All those many places you've visited stop returning pleasure. You are a little weary, and you are ready for your steps to lead back home.

Home is never just foundation, walls, windows, doors, rooms, roofs. Never just a house, shelter, a space to occupy or simply stop

27

by. We ask of the front door to home, "Does the key fit easily into the lock?" That might be the most telltale sign of a welcoming home and a welcome home committee. They furnished you with the right key, and they kept the lock smooth and working.

Home nurses and nourishes. Home is a sling when your arm's broken, the comfortable chair in the family room— your spot for healing. It is the first place an infant rests, reposes.

Home and hope. Hope and home. One letter difference. How close otherwise? Home perishes when hope flies out the windows, when love exits by the back door, when acceptance is washed clean with the laundry, when angels are barred from entrance, when peace is no longer the way forward, but only a forwarded address on the other side of town, when the politics of anger slips into the house through a side door.

And home perishes when lace curtains no longer frame a carefully-chosen flowerpot in front of the window sill, when a family no longer sits down together for a meal, when a candle that used to be lit for display in a welcoming front window no longer is brought out of the cupboard, when friends no longer feel welcomed — anytime, for any reason, when poison is at home in the house instead of in the work shed, when trouble finds a home there, when the place has become a hiding place and a fortress of protection against the outside community.

Home has space for secrets and love, lies and games, devils and angels, pretending and learning, complaints against the world, and mismatched socks, and patterned china.

Home is a bookcase of poems, stories, plays, essays, memoirs, histories that take care of us, teach us, lead us out of our homes to the world. For the world is home; it is where we make life, make friends, meet partners, build communities, shape our personalities. "Every day is a journey, and the journey itself is home."

A Baptist Praying in a Blue Dress
by Carole Ann Crateau

It was 1956, the final week of school. Dust particles floated aimlessly on June sunbeams. With our social studies books open, we were staring out the windows. What page was that?

Eighth grade graduation was just days away. All we could think of was diving into Wildcat Lake in our new bathing suits. One after another, squeals of pure shock echoed across the water.

"Carole," Miss Copley motioned me to her desk.

Blanche Copley was strict but fair and even liked us most of the time. "Carole, you've been chosen to give the eighth grade invocation at graduation." I guess she assumed my silence was a "yes." She added, "Be sure to jot down your prayer on a 3 x 5 note card—just in case. It doesn't have to be long."

Praying in front of people! I'd never done that before. Besides, Miss Copley didn't realize that I was a Baptist or that it mattered. Write my prayer! Baptists don't write their prayers like "liberal" Methodists and Presbyterians. They stay open to the Spirit's leading—nothing *canned* about Baptist prayers. I learned in Sunday school how to pray off the cuff, from the heart—the Baptist way.

Of course, I would not need a 3 x 5 card. I was sure that the right phrases would come to me in the moment. Pastor Hanson always closed his eyes when he prayed. It was natural to talk to God without reading anything. Anyway, I didn't feel like practicing. God would think it kind of phony—like the Catholics with their repetition. This would be Dewey Junior High's largest graduation. Nothing could prepare me for this crowd.

The next few days sped by. I shopped for several hours in search of the right dress. Finally, I found my dream at Anita's dress shop. A bit more expensive than I'd planned, but it was worth it. I promised myself that "I'd work on the prayer a little later, one thing at a time." Soon enough, it was time.

Our principal, Mr. Stewart, opened the ceremony that afternoon in his booming voice. Then he sat down. I was next to stand on the podium, a large rectangle of risers. Behind the microphone, I gazed out to the eighth grade girls and older guys: some so cool they were every girl's dream. Never had Dewey Junior High gymnasium held so many folding chairs and people. Now all eyes were riveted on me. There I stood in my sky blue cotton sateen dress with white polka dots the size of quarters. The bodice was snug with a wide white collar and the skirt flounced to the max with three layers of netted slips.

I was overcome, speechless, searching for a word, any word. Silence grew on itself until I thought my heart had stopped. I could barely breathe. Miss Copley whispered, almost hissing: "Just say SOMEthing, ANYthing." I trusted her.

But now, standing alone on the podium, even Miss Copley couldn't help me. My brain drew a blank and the Spirit—where did it go? It must have checked out, too. Chairs squeaked as people rearranged themselves. A few men gave hearty coughs to fill the air space. Women fidgeted with their gloves and purses. In the second row below me, I noticed Mom and Dad staring at their shoes. They never went to church or prayed; this was out of their league.

"Dear God," I fumbled into the mike.

Then words skittered like raindrops in a gusty wind.

"Help us all. Help us . . . help us to call on you when we need help." My blush rose from pink to magenta. The air was growing warm and stuffy with the faint odor of gym socks. I looked down at the folds of my skirt scattered with polka dots. I didn't dare search for familiar friends, afraid to see the horror or was that amusement on their faces?

And, as an afterthought, I blurted, "Thank you. Amen."

As I uttered the Amen, a collective sigh rose up. I turned to sit beside Miss Copley. She patted my knee and smiled, undaunted by disaster, while I looked down, folding my hands on my lap to still my nervous shaking. After the painfully long ceremony, a few parents and neighbors thanked me for their "moment of silence." My Sunday school teacher, Mr. Davidson, shook my hand, a big smile on his Baptist face. If he could see the humor, I could breathe again.

***

Students were busy making plans. Bill Stotts found me in the crowd.

"Hey Carole, Dave Alfred is throwing a party, want to come?"

Would I? I had friends all right, but never figured out what it took to fit in with the popular crowd. Not surprising, I had never been invited to a boy-girl party. Here was a breakthrough, thanks to Bill, someone I barely noticed in my Social Studies class. The party guy, Dave, just lived across the street from the school. I found my parents and got an easy approval to stay for a couple hours.

Little did I know those two hours would raise my awareness of all that I had been missing. The familiar rock and roll beat was pounding the air waves as we neared the Alfred house. Mrs. Alfred greeted us and pointed to plates of cookies on the table. I don't know where she went, but she disappeared just like that. This was new territory—no parents.

"Carole!" greeted Dolores, standing in a corner with a couple guys on the basketball team. She was always quick with the tease. "Guess what I heard?" I looked her way as she whispered in her loud voice, "Some guys say you're built like a brick shithouse."

"What's that?" I asked, oblivious, but not giving her room to taunt me.

"Yours to find out," she boasted. A few older guys smiled an in-the-know look.

Bill and I followed the crowd into the hallway leading to the living room, definitely no parents here! The steady couples were sitting crammed together on the living room couch, lost in eternal hugs while "Only You" was playing.

The tall guys were congratulating the girls with long-locked kisses on their lips. I was swept into the tide, a line-up of older boys who had never spoken to me before now in command with the awkward three-step: first, grab and hug; second, tip her; and third, plant the kiss with fervent lips. Strange but captivating. At thirteen, I had never been kissed by a boy before. Now I lost count. I was taking lessons for the "Party Girl."

There was a certain pattern here of tight, determined lips, demanding more than they could hope for in one brief moment.

Bill and I veered off into another room where ten or twelve were sitting in a circle on the floor with a spinning bottle in the center. "Hey Carole, want to play?" grinned Denny White. Every emotion from embarrassment to thrill was hitting the jackpot.

"Sure." I was open for a risk.

This was a game for people who liked to kiss just about anyone. Fats Domino was singing, "Ain't That a Shame?" But it wasn't really. Silly and embarrassing, maybe, but it wasn't a shame. After several spins, I noticed that the bottle could be directed towards a certain guy or girl. Truly, it was not a game of chance. If it didn't stop at my feet fairly often, my kissable rating would drop like a brick. I decided that I preferred the random, endless kissing where you didn't take time to think about the guy you just kissed.

I was spinning the bottle when someone shouted, "Hey Carole, your dad's here." The bottle twirled crazily and finally pointed to brainy Norm Johnston's feet. Poor guy was looking as awkward as I felt. His mom worked in the fabric department at J.C. Penney's. Would she, could she, ever imagine her Norman in this kissing frenzy?

"Oh, my dad's here, Norm. Sorry." I was tired of kissing anyway, smiled a thanks to Norm, and headed for the door. Bill caught up with me as I found the way out. Good thing Dad was waiting for me in the car and didn't come to the Alfreds' door.

"Can I write you?" Bill asked as he walked along beside me. He was leaving soon with his family. His dad was being stationed on some lonely atoll in the middle of the Pacific which is the problem of living in a Navy town.

As he helped me pile folds of netting and sky blue skirt with polka dots into our family's low-slung Hudson, I answered, "Sure." I'd write him back. Come to think, we never even kissed that wild night.

As far as I can remember.

Honey
by Kay Gerard

Honey, I have stories to tell.
Of course I do.
I could tell you about all those years in East Texas.
You can see the scars on my hands.
I could talk about cotton
and outdoor toilets
and what your grandma had to endure
in those fields with those boss men.

But that's my past. It's gone.

What about right now,
right here in Salem, Oregon?

Why just last week I was walking downtown,
in the middle of the day, when I saw
a young woman walking pretty fast
towards me on the sidewalk.
Her dark eyes wide, her face full of fear.
A young man was right behind her, maybe

six or eight feet.
I don't know what he was thinking, and
I don't know what he was saying.
But I just slowed down right in front
of her and looked her in the eyes.
She had to stop.

I took both of her hands and said,
"Honey, I haven't seen you for so long.
How've you been?
How's your family?"

She looked up at me,
and I held her hands until she took a good breath
and that young nuisance walked right on by.

"Oh, thank you," she whispered, "thank you."

The Home of the Brave

by Kay Gerard

after Penina Ava Taesali

Oh say, can you see?

Our Lady of Sorrows
Her cheeks drowning in tears.
Her arms reaching down to hold us.

Her grandfather chased off without pay.
Her grandmother choked on insecticides.

Her son's brown skin stamped with a false nationality
As the gun is aimed.

Her daughter's persistence torn from her hands
Like a stained dollar bill.

Her eagle's nests torched in flames.

At the twilight's last gleaming
What do we proudly hail?

Not the land of the free.

But surely the home of the brave.
Pray for us, Our Lady.

Online Dating
By Gayle McMurria-Bachik

It was late one evening when I laid aside the magazine article extolling the benefits of online dating. Throwing back the rest of my gin and tonic, I turned to my kitty Selma and asked, "Do you think I should consider dating again?"

Selma mewed as if to say, "Why"? In turn, I reminded her that even though I was sixty-nine years old, I had aged pretty well, and I think I could carry on a decent conversation with a stranger. Why shouldn't I invite a little romance into my life, or at least just a little male companionship?

Wyatt has been dead for three years. Although he told me to find someone after he was gone, I don't think he meant it. Well, maybe he did. I am a bit lonely. My married friends encourage me to hang out with them, but mostly I am just fine on my own. I have Selma, my sweet kitty. I have my garden. And, I have my gin and tonic for long, cold, lonely evenings.

OMG! Did I really think that? Am I really that lame? Am I spending too many long evenings snuggling with Selma watching reruns on the Hallmark romance channel? Yeah. Well okay, I might as well check out some dating websites. What could it hurt? After all, my friend's son met his wife on E-Harmony and she says, "They're as compatible as two peas in a pod."

They say online dating is safe, and anyone can find a compatible match. Maybe. It certainly has to be quicker and less awkward than chatting up that good-looking guy I see at AJ's Hideaway from time to time. His name is George, I think. Not that I am looking for another Mr. Right. Once in a lifetime seems about all a reasonable woman can expect. However, I could do with a little manly company from time to time.

Because it's free, I'll start with *Match-Made-in-Heaven.* Good grief! Completing their form was more challenging and emotionally exhausting than I could have ever imagined. It took me hours and hours. As they all say, the more completely and accurately you answer the questions, the more likely you will find the perfect match.

After answering the basic questions like gender, age, and education, their probes morphed into personal interests and lifestyle categories.

Do you like to read? Yes, lots. Especially cozy mysteries and historical fiction. I have belonged to the same book club for thirty years.

Do you exercise? I walk and take classes at the gym (unless a good excuse comes up).

Do you like movies? Art house films like the kind that play at Salem Cinema, but nothing violent. Recently I loved the *RBG* (I think this answer would be a good spoiler alert for my political values, unless the reader doesn't know who RBG is.)

Do you like theater? Yes, I loved attending Pentacle Theater, Oregon Shakespeare Festival, and Portland Center Stage with my husband when he was alive—not so much by myself.

What kind of music do you like? You name it, I like it. Mostly, I lean toward classical standards and crooners from the 50's and 60's for just listening, but a good honky-tonk or hip-hop tune can get me bopping.

What is your favorite art? Anything done by my granddaughter, southwestern artists like R.C. Gorman and Frank Howell, and artists who make stunning political statements.

Some questions really made me think about the values and personal characteristics that matter most to me. Such as, would I consider dating a Republican? Probably not.

As relentless a process as that was, it turned out to be a quickie compared to the time it took to choose a picture to attach to the questionnaire. After much deliberation, I finally picked a snapshot that was a bit recent and which highlighted my finer points (or so I hoped). Wyatt always said he liked that picture. (I admit I was tempted to use a professional shot from twenty years ago. Second thoughts along the line of truth-in-lending hacked that desire.)

Since I put so much effort into that website questionnaire, I decided to submit an application to a couple of others, hoping to increase my odds of getting a match. Then I waited. I hadn't dated for thirty-six years! What am I supposed to do if I agree to meet some guy?

Stealth study!

Yes, while I wait to see if a match pings up on my computer, I'll go to AJ's Hideaway to observe local dating behavior. I had been there a few times in the past to have their perfectly cooked prime rib and had felt safe, and I enjoyed its neglected fifties ambience.

Walking in from a sunny afternoon, I removed my sunglasses and blinked a few times to adjust to the darkened room. Nodding to a waitress I recognized, I smiled tentatively at the customers who were sitting around as I found a stool at the bar to focus on my mission.

My plan was to discreetly watch couple behavior while not appearing to stalk them. Several twosomes nursed their beverage of choice without much conversation. Once in a while they would speak to each other over the din of the TV and jukebox racket. I think I can handle this. I'll just meet my match in a darkened room with loud music. I won't have to talk much. But there have to be some rules. I jotted down a few from the magazine article I read:

> **Rule 1**: Go Dutch. I pay my own way. I don't want my perfect match to think I owe him something.
> **Rule 2:** The first date should be chaperoned, but from a discrete distance. I'll ask a friend to be my

lookout. If I want out, I'll give her a sign, like, I'll start plucking the hairs on my chin. Then she will call my cell phone, and I'll make a speedy retreat.

Rule 3: I only drink one gin and tonic, no matter how fast I consume it.

I hadn't noticed that George had come in and sat down on the bar seat beside me.

"Making your grocery list?" he asked.

I don't know what came over me. His question so surprised me, I actually told him what I was doing. Instead of laughing, he volunteered to be my "lookout" if I brought any of my matches to AJ's. That was unexpected, but why not? I could use a "wing man" so to speak, and the entire bar staff seemed to like him.

I was genuinely surprised when I got some "hits." I read and re-read the bios and inspected the pictures suspiciously. (After all, I had *almost* attached a deceptively young picture of myself.)

"Our Time," a dating site for fifty-plus singles found me a match named Terry, a fisherman from the coast. He was white-haired and a bit shorter than me, but buff (really buff), if the picture was accurate. He was divorced, had three grown kids and offered to supply me with a lifetime of fresh fish. He liked walking on the beach at sunset.

We arranged to meet the following Sunday for a buffet at the Spirit Mountain Casino, between Newport and Salem. He was a nice man, and I liked the way he went on about his grandchildren, very devoted. But no sparks flew between us.

The second ping was from Match.com. Gerald (do not call him Jerry) sounded pretty interesting. His photo showed a very tall, lean guy, a former university professor, retired and never married. He liked French cuisine, and it seemed he traveled a lot. He also liked long walks on the beach. (What? Is that a coincidence or reaction to something I said on my questionnaire?)

Coffee at the French Press was his suggestion for a meeting place. I didn't mention I hated coffee, but I knew they had a killer hot chai. He was sitting at a table reading when I arrived. A perfect gentleman, he closed his book and stood up when I introduced myself. He ordered his favorite coffee for me even though I repeated several times I would rather have tea. Maybe he was hard of hearing?

His first words were to ask what I was reading. I started to tell him about *A Gentleman in Moscow* by Amor Towles. He listened for a nanosecond and picked up the book from the table: *Anna Karenina*. Gerald condescendingly informed me he had just finished re-reading the complete works of Count Lyov Nikolayevich Tolstoy and pointed out that the author is usually referred to in English as Leo Tolstoy, the Russian writer who is regarded as one of the greatest authors of all time.

Okay, that was noteworthy. Then, he lectured me on the import-tance of Tolstoy's major works. I hadn't attempted to read Tolstoy since college. I tried to be a good listener, nodded from time to time, and pasted a look of interest on my face. (I began wishing my wingman was in the room.) When he asked me to remind him of my name, he suggested we meet again. I promised I would check my calendar. I'm such a liar.

Third time's the charm, right? Following on the heels of Gerald came Frank. At his suggestion we met at the Silver Spur Bar off Portland Road for a drink. He was dressed totally in black western wear, including a black ten-gallon cowboy hat and a black Martin guitar. There was something familiar about that look, but I couldn't put my finger on it until he picked up the guitar, strumming a bit and started singing Johnny Cash's *"Man in Black."*

Wide-eyed I looked around the room, but other customers seemed uninterested in this little show. But I was really taken aback and not sure what to think. I like Johnny Cash, and appreciate the social value of his ballad's lyrics. But this guy was no Johnny Cash, although the guitar was really cool. He was way over the top. No second dates here.

Back at A.J.'s, I sat down next to George. He looked over and ordered a gin and tonic for me and said, "The first one's on me." After a few minutes, he asked me how the computer dating was going and would he ever get to be my wingman? I had debriefed him after the first couple of "match dates" and would entertain him with some of the more hilarious or uncomfortable moments.

He was always genuinely interested and made lots of consoling comments like, "what a jerk." It had become easy to talk with George. He was a good listener and quick to recognize when my stories needed a chuckle, a full-out laugh, or a sympathetic comment. When he asked about my most recent adventure, I told him I was done with finding the perfect match. "I'm ready to get back on my couch with Selma."

"But you still have one more date to schedule," he said.

"Not really," I said, "I pulled my profile from every website. So, I'm really done."

He smiled. "But there is *one* more. You still need to go out with me."

Best match ever.

Beauty, Smoke, and the Thing with Feathers
by Molly Dinsdale

If you believe what scientists tell us: that birds are what became of dinosaurs, then you can really access some hope—as long as you know that it's really long-term hope. And what a deliriously enchanting outcome—T Rexes into Peregrine falcons, Brontosauri into dabbling ducks, Velociraptors into hummingbirds. Possibly humans could evolve in this way into creatures living in harmony with the world around them. Part of diversity. Diverseness recognized and prized as an expression of true health and imagination, while sameness is seen as the unstable, unhealthy fragile, inviting invasion and species wars for dominance. We might see ourselves as part of the amazing diversity, part of the complex balance and gradual shifts that allow all life forms the time to intertwine and evolve.

We humans get these gifts, amazing gifts, often so hard to recognize at the time. What of water? What of trees, forested valleys, hard granite transformed from an ancient river of stone?

Our plane flew over the valley, a beautiful still day, over the upland farms, the cottonwoods telling us of the secret meanderings of creeks, of the dominating presence of the big rivers. As it was spring, the drive home spoke rhododendron and daffodil—this *is* the Garden of Eden, this rivered ecosystem. I felt some portion of ecstasy to be re-entering the green garden of the valley in April.

***

Cut to late August with plumes of smoke along the entirety of the Cascades. Smoke spread out, eclipsing the white topped mountains, our barometer of water availability obscured. Some say the world will end in fire: countless trees, ferns, mosses, owls, warblers, wrens, muskrats, deer, frogs, butterflies are no longer here to attest to that one way or another. Bringing us to the questions—how resilient are they? I think of the Carolina parakeet—yes, we did have a beautiful, noisy parakeet—it was this, it was that: nesting trees chopped down for firewood, wood islands with the right berries cleared for a little farm, a stylish hat needing feathers—and so they disappeared from planet Earth. Without Audubon, we would know nothing of their wild and raucous beauty. And so *it, they, we* go—leaving a soft and stunning memory of wildness, of beauty, of the unique music of each and a glimpse of their place in the light of our slow growing understanding of the Web of Life.

I am accepting the coming of fall, the dark morning with its cold rain quenching the devouring fires of late summer bringing the smoky particulates down to earth again. I walk out into the dripping woods appreciating the wateriness of the rain and wish the same for all of California. Some feel that our state is superior to that of our glittery, glitzy, wine-and-silicon-filled neighbor to the south. And I'm part of that cohort, really liking the idea that my state is not yet too big on the notorious or glitz radar. I wonder at the fires that have come into our world, not the immediate and horror-filled tragedy of a bomb in a crowded town, but overwhelming and devastating none the less.

What do each of these bringers of fire mean for today, tomorrow but most achingly, for who we are as a species and what we can do to ourselves and each other? Fire in terms of warm hearths, genial wood stoves, bringer of warm air to sodden leaf rakers or freezing snowman builders, crackles in fierce paradox to the unleashed and capricious force even the gods cannot tame.

Yes, we love the natural world—we are becoming more careful with the tinder of our campfires, more conscious of the maxims that we are in a complex web of dependency, that we are all downstream, that there are consequences to what we extract, and cut down and burn because it's all connected. But what of our word *tinder*, our word *gasoline*? I huddle in my little world, lift the phone to register my alarm to my representatives, write letters, work on a salt marsh, recycle, feeling lame as I do this, tiny before powerful gods. I reach back to ordinary comforts that once seemed to hold the sense of a grounded and good reality that could really hold a barrier and an answer to the chaos of the political and the dim, dumb incremental but accelerating decline of our only home.

Still, there sometimes is a rare and majestic perspective, as when the moon passes in front of the sun. Gathered on a small hilltop, the country roads lined with fellow watchers, we sat, tiny beings in the changing light, joined so wonderfully with thousands staring with the awe of all humans on planet Earth at the elemental coming and going and coming of the light. An unexpected happiness of community seemed to alter the chaotic forces pulling us apart, insight was granted, and for a moment we heard clearly the music of the spheres.

Resupply
by Molly Dinsdale

Scotland's Torridon Highlands: Looking at the guide book the call was clear, beautiful, beckoning—and we answered. Driving along the rivered valley, we looked for a path. There were no signs anywhere, no parking lot, no map kiosk, just wild hills running upwards from the glaciated valley.

Finally, a small stone marker suggested a possible way up—a subtle invitation that transformed slowly into a true stone stairway, and we hobbit-like ascended. Was it a natural stair? An old mountain dwarf construction leading to a treasure cavern? A secret escape route to the unseen valleys on the other side?

We clambered up in silent conversation with each other and the place. Below, we could see occasional tiny cars and the classic ribbon of river winding around the base of a great hill and out of sight. There were magical-seeming rocks of multicolor and sparkles, chartreuse and orange lichens in fairy circles on slabs of granite frozen in a flow of long ago. Suddenly, a cleft appeared with hidden waterfall and one late October foxglove. No one said much, but we communed.

At last, the ridge top and sheer walls dropped away speaking of past ages and old lore. Surely, this was a secret route of old clans. Surely, the pastures far below us were once a lovely and secure kingdom made safe by the Torridon Cliffs—a true mountain fastness.

In hardly a breath of wind, we ate our cheese and apples and breathed in the high air and gazed: the yearning idea of an escape, a safe place, a shelter palpable before us. At bay was the ineffably complex, the intractable, the heartbreaking, the demanding, the inexorable. And the gift of resupply to our cache of awareness, imagination, hope, energy for the tasks ahead was granted.

Gift Exchange
by Jean Rover

Let's just say I couldn't stand Margaret Skinner.

Tall and slim with sleek dark hair, she always crowded in line at school like she was somebody. Plus, she had all those dresses her lawyer daddy bought her from Bertha's Boutique. Not to mention, she made fun of my brown oxfords and my thin, white anklets that never rolled down right. So, I thought I would just *die* when I drew her name in our third grade Christmas gift exchange.

Margaret Skinner. Of all people.

Daddy drove Mom and me to town in our brown DeSoto and dropped us off at Della's Variety and Dime so we could shop. Della's was packed with so much Christmas stuff, my eyes popped. I wanted to look at everything—yo-yos, all kinds of colored beads you could string, and cute little bottles of red and pink nail polish I wasn't allowed to wear. I couldn't help it. I grabbed the long, sleek handle of the one called *Hot Strawberry*.

"Mom, can I—"

"Put it back and don't dawdle," Mom said. "We can't afford that. Daddy's just going to get some gas and then be back to pick us up. Find something for Margaret."

Hmmm. What could I get her? Heck, she already had dozens of those pretty little plastic barrettes which her well-behaved hair didn't even need.

Finally, I suggested we get Margaret some Fleer's Double Bubble gum or Kiwi shoe cleaner that came in a little tin for her fancy saddle shoes. That would be good enough for uppity Margaret.

"It's Christmas, Cassie," Mom said. "Get something nice." She pointed me to a little pile of jack sets. Each package had ten silver jacks with a red rubber ball smack in the center. What really caught my eye was the plastic ballerina charm hooked to the package with a chain. She stood on one toe, her arms in the air, and her hair piled on top of her head. I dreamed of being a ballerina, gliding across some big city stage to wild applause.

"Those are nice," I said, feeling a jealous pang in my stomach that she would want Margaret to have one. *What about me?*

All Mom said was, "Hurry and pick one. You know how impatient Daddy gets when we keep him waiting."

I chose the set with a pink ballerina charm. Afterward, Mom bought a big roll of red wrapping paper covered with jolly Santas and candy canes. I hoped that meant that me and my brother, Rodney, would be getting lots of gifts.

At home, Mom said it was my job to wrap Margaret's gift. She placed the wrapping paper, some clear tape, my blunt-tipped scissors, and a ball of red yarn on the kitchen table. I cut a paper square and placed the jack set in the middle. I couldn't help thinking. *This is just too good for ol' Margaret.* So, before I folded and taped the paper, I slipped the chain and the ballerina off and slid it into my pocket. Then I finished the package off with a stringy yarn bow.

Take that, Margaret Skinner.

At school, we placed all the presents under the tree we'd decorated with colored paper chains, snowmen, and bells we'd made in art class. I loved working with that big jar of white paste and glitter. I put glitter on everything.

Later that week, the room mothers arrived with a whole bunch of gingerbread cookies, candy canes, and pink punch. Afterward, Randy Byers and Vickie Nelson were selected to hand out the gifts. I got a tiny heart-shaped bottle of Blue Waltz perfume from Marsha Harlan. Wow. I couldn't wait. I undid the small cap and dabbed a few drops behind my earlobes. Pow! I was powdery-sweet Cinderella on the way to the ball. I couldn't thank Marsha enough. I mean perfume for crying out loud.

The chatter stopped when Mrs. Case rapped on her desk with her ruler to make an announcement. "Could everyone please look around their desks? Margaret says something from her gift has fallen off and is missing. Now what was it exactly Margaret?"

Margaret stood there with her arms folded across her chest. "I seen these jack packs at Della's. They all come with a charm. Mine is missing."

My face got hot. My eyes locked on my desk top. I didn't count on her noticing. Everyone was crawling on the floor searching for nothing. I thought I'd better join in. So I scrambled to the floor, too.

I was so-o-o glad when the bell rang, and we all got dismissed early for Christmas break. I snuck a peek at Margaret. She looked like she could use a good dose of baking soda.

I hurriedly packed my stuff and dashed toward the coat rack. I had one arm in my wool jacket when I felt a tap on the shoulder. I turned.

Margaret!

She slowly wound the red yarn from my package around her thumb; then pulled it off and tossed it on the floor. "Was there a ballerina on the jack set when you bought it?" she asked, her voice cold.

I couldn't look her in the eye. "I didn't buy it," I said, studying her shoes. "My mom did. She picked it out and wrapped it."

Margaret's mouth puckered like she'd swallowed a pickle. "I'm going to go to Della's and find out," she said, tapping the floor with her newly scuffed saddle shoe. "Della should take this back and give me a proper one. It's not right."

I wished then that we'd gotten the shoe cleaner.

As I headed for the door, I heard Margaret say, "Who wraps packages with yarn?" Then, she made a noise with her mouth that sounded like she'd cut loose.

Was what I did stealing? I didn't dare ask Rodney. He'd blab to Mom. And, I had kinda lied. Weren't there commandments in the Bible about stealing and lying? On the other hand, I did give Margaret a gift like I was supposed to—just not all of it.

At home, I reached into my pocket to sneak peeks at the plastic ballerina. Every time I did, I glanced over my shoulder. It would be easy for Margaret to get to the dime store because she lived in town.

Would Della say that we'd bought a jack set? Would she tell Margaret? Would Mom remember what was attached to it? Best to keep it hidden. I tucked the charm into my underwear drawer, piled on a few socks and a comic book for good measure. Taking the ballerina was so easy, but that night I couldn't sleep. In the morning, I could hardly eat. Jeez, not liking someone was harder than I thought. Maybe I should ask God to forgive me. Would He?

***

Baking cookies with Mom was a fun thing we did every Christmas. The cookies made the whole house smell like vanilla, and they looked lovely arranged on Mom's glass tray. What I didn't like was going with her to deliver a plate to the Widow Carothers. She was a crotchety old woman with a hump on her back who lived up the road in a faded green shake house. The blinds were always drawn, she called me Cassandra instead of Cassie, and she complained. Her back hurt. Her knee was giving out. The colored sprinkles I put on her cookies stuck to her teeth. The raisins in the oatmeal ones were dry. The boys in the neighborhood left muddy bike tracks in front of her mail box. Did Rodney have a bike? Why didn't Mom do something about my unruly brown curls?

"Land sakes," she'd croak and feel my hair. "Looks like you're haulin' a brush pile on your head." Then she'd laugh like that was supposed to be funny.

What about her hair? It was greasy and tied up on her head in a wispy knot, and she smelled like Vicks.

"I don't want to go with you, Mom," I said. "Mrs. Carothers is an old grump. Besides, she doesn't appreciate anything. Just gripes. And the tea she makes us is lukewarm."

Mom shook her finger. "Shame on you, Cassandra Mills. Such talk. There's no duty in giving her a gift."

I licked the mixing spoon. "She can't even say *thank you*. All she does is babble about what's wrong with everything."

Mom gave me one of her looks. "It's not easy being old. Your body aches, your family is gone, most of your friends have died, and you can't get out much. I would guess she'd be mighty happy to have a few cheerful cookies when she wakes up on Christmas morning in that drafty house of hers all alone."

"Maybe she could get a cat," I suggested.

Mom's eyebrows went up and then settled into a frown. "You know what? The best part of giving someone something is not the thing itself, but what it does to you. Inside, I mean. Mrs. Carothers can mutter, scowl, throw the cookies out. It doesn't matter. What matters is this warm glow I feel right here." She put her hands to her chest. "A gift is a way of caring. Haven't you felt that when you've been nice to someone?"

I couldn't look at her. My *insides* lurched remembering the pink plastic ballerina was upstairs in my room hidden under a pile of my underpants.

***

"Don't rip and tear," Mom cautioned us Christmas morning. "That way we can save the wrapping paper and use it again."

Rodney got a new baseball mitt, underwear, and a bottle of Vitalis Tonic to slick his hair. I got a pogo stick and two yards of emerald green corduroy, so Mom could make me that jumper I'd been wanting. Mom said when her egg money came in next week, we could go to Della's and pick out a pattern. She'd have the jumper sewed up before school started again.

I held the soft, green fabric to my face. That's when a third thing dropped out—a small package of jacks with a white ballerina charm! My heart stopped. Now, I had two ballerina charms.

"What's the matter, Cassie?" Mom asked. "I thought you wanted jacks. I mean that day in the store—"

"I ... uh ... " I got up and threw my arms around her to stop her questions. "Thank you. Thank you."

Later that day, Grandma and Grampa Owen came to our house for a turkey dinner with all the trimmings. Grandma brought two pies, pumpkin and blueberry, and bags of candy for Rodney and me— Junior Mints, Dad's Root Beer Barrels and my favorite, Tootsie Rolls. I could hardly eat. *Was it stealing to take something before you actually gave it?*

Mom looked at my barely touched plate. She felt my forehead. "I do believe she's coming down with something."

51

***

When school started again in January, I snuck in the classroom early wearing my green jumper. Mrs. Case was sitting at her desk. I wasn't counting on her being there.

She glanced at her watch. "My goodness, you're early" she said. "What a lovely jumper. I assume you had a nice holiday?"

"Yeah," I assured her. "Did you?" She droned on and on about her relatives, what they ate, all the places they went, the traffic, the weather. I was getting antsy.

Finally, Mrs. Case took a breath. I saw my chance. "I need to go to the bathroom."

She smiled. "Sure, go right ahead."

When I came back, Mrs. Case was busy shuffling through papers. I quickly dropped the ballerina and chain on top of Margaret's desk just as the bell rang. I slid into my seat and waited, trying to think what I'd say when Margaret found it. Would she accuse me?

Nose-in-the-air Margaret strolled in showing off her new, white plastic purse that looked like a wicker basket. None of us girls in the third grade carried purses.

"Hey," she said, when she reached her desk, "What's this? My ballerina charm! I went to Della's to get a new jack set, but she was all sold out."

Mrs. Case stood and smoothed her skirt. She shot me a look.

I turned my head toward the windows pretending I'd spotted something interesting out there, all the time my ears burning.

"How'd it get here?" Margaret asked.

Mrs. Case cleared her throat. "Uh, the janitor must have found your missing charm when he cleaned the floor."

I snuck a peek at Margaret who was grinning like a monkey. She fastened the ballerina to her white purse like it was meant to be. She didn't say any more. Neither did Mrs. Case.

I felt a mountain lift off my body. And, to be honest, I felt a little glow creep into my chest like Mom said. Not much of one being it was Margaret, but just enough to get the idea.

Contributors

Carole Ann Crateau: Carole Ann Crateau has lived in Salem since 1971. She taught creative writing at Oregon State University for fourteen years. She says, "I found my place in the world with pen and ink."

Molly Dinsdale:
Mother of four,
Psychotherapist,
Gardener,
Rower and walker,
Travel arounder, and lover of dear people, reading, and wildness, exuberance, imagination, diversity, and generosity.

Sara Dinsdale grew up in a large family on a western Oregon farm and has traveled extensively, providing her with a wealth of story starters.

Gayle McMurria-Bachik wants her husband to know she has never personally utilized the services of a dating website, but has interviewed many friends who have had similar experiences. Before retiring from the Oregon Department of Education, Gayle was fortunate to be an education coordinator for the Family Head Start program, the last surviving program of the War on Poverty.

Nancy Fischer credits her creativity to her Irish-Italian heritage, the Pacific Northwest, children and grandchildren, middle school students, nature's mysteries, and Jack, who still makes her laugh.

Marge French writes because she likes to and enjoys the group. She is a retired English as a Second Language teacher and lives in Salem, Oregon with Mr. Willaby, her cat.

Kay Gerard has spent most of her life on the west coast, loves libraries, and is grateful to her friends who write so she that she has more to read.

Lois Rosen joyfully leads Salem's Trillium Writers and the ICL Writers group at Willamette University. A co-founder of the Peregrine Poets, she's won Willamette Writers' 2016 Kay Snow Fiction Award and had her story performed and recorded by the Portland Liars' League. Her poetry books are *Pigeons* (Traprock Books) and *Nice and Loud* (Tebot Bach). Her work has been published in over 100 magazines and online. She's taught English as a Second Language in Oregon, New York, Japan, Ecuador, Colombia, and Costa Rica.

Jean Rover's short fiction was performed at Liars' League events in London, England and Portland, Oregon. Another story, *The Day Truman Ruined Our Jam,* was included in the *Saturday Evening Post's* Great American Fiction Contest 2018 Anthology. Others have been recognized by *Writer's Digest* and Oregon Writers Colony and published in various literary journals. Her chapbook, *Beneath the Boughs Unseen*, features holiday stories about society's invisible people.

Karen Runkel:
Childhood: a reader, a writer.
College: a degree in journalism.
At work: ad copy, press releases.
Later: editing, personal essays published.
Now: freedom to explore.

Paul Suter grew up in the San Francisco Bay Area. He settled in Salem in 1973 and today focuses on writing, activism, and copy-editing *The PeaceWorker*.

www.ingramcontent.com/pod-product-compliance
Lightning Source LLC
Chambersburg PA
CBHW071210130626
46555CB00004B/1658